TO
CAROLYN -

ALWAYS LET "HOPE" LEAD
         YOUR JOURNEY.
                    Bill Kiley

www.mascotbooks.com

Hope and Freckles: *Fleeing to a Better Forest*

Kiley Press, LLC
www.kileypress.com

Kiley Press, LLC is a registered trademark.
Text and illustrations copyright 2020 by
Kiley Press, LLC

Kiley Press provides special discounts when purchased in larger volumes for premiums and promotional purposes, as well as for fundraising and educational use.

For more information:
www.HopeAndFreckles.com

For more information, please contact:
Mascot Books
620 Herndon Parkway #320
Herndon, VA 20170
info@mascotbooks.com

Library of Congress Control Number: 2019912065

CPSIA Code: PRT1219B
ISBN-13: 978-1-64543-254-8

Printed in the United States

Hope and Freckles

Fleeing to a Better Forest

Written by **Bill Kiley**   Illustrated by **Mary Manning**

Hope had lived in the Olden Forest all of her life. She had even brought her baby boy, Freckles, into the world there. She loved the forest and loved watching Freckles grow up there, but something was changing.

The summers were
getting hotter, there
was less water available,
and the plants were
drying up. Hope had to spend
more and more time looking for food. And
when she looked, she feared for the safety of
her fawn and herself.

Jaguars and coyotes were prowling about, always searching
for their prey. There was even talk of hunters being seen in
the forest. Hope knew the Olden Forest
wouldn't be safe for much longer.

"Freckles," said Hope, "we have to leave our home and find a safer place to live. It'll be a long walk, but it will be beautiful and I'll stay right by your side. The Big Pine Forest will be a perfect new home for us."

And so, Hope and Freckles said goodbye to their family and friends and began their long trip, walking by day and sleeping by night. Along the way, they encountered other families that were fleeing the dangers of other forests, and together they traveled to find refuge.

When they finally reached the Big Pine Forest,
they were surprised to find a long, tall fence
surrounding it. They followed the fence until
they found a big gate and two guards.

"Hello," said Hope to the guards.
"We've traveled all the way from the
Olden Forest in search of a safer
home. Can we come into the
Big Pine Forest?"

"No one is allowed in," said one
guard. "We already have enough
white-tailed deer living in the
forest. We don't want any more."

"Besides," said the other guard,
"you might have ticks and insects
on your fur, and you could make the
deer who live here sick."

"But we walked such a long way from our forest to get here," said Hope, pulling Freckles closer to her. "My fawn is so tired from the journey. Can't we stay just for a little while to rest and get some food and water?"

"I don't think so," said the guard. "You just want to eat our food and do nothing to earn it. That's probably why you came anyway."

"I came for the safety of my fawn," said Hope strongly. "We were running out of food and water in the Olden Forest, and we were being hunted. I am afraid to go back. Please, let us in."

"Please, sir," said Freckles. "I want to be safe with my momma."

The two guards looked at each other. Then one said, "Wait out here. We will check to see what we can do."

The sun began to set and the deer laid down on the ground and began to fall asleep.

The next day, the guards came back and told Hope that she, Freckles, and the other families could come into the beautiful forest, but only for a little while. "You also have to stay in a fenced-in area until the General, who's in charge of the Big Pine Forest, decides if you can live there."

Freckles looked at his mother and said, "Let's go, Momma!"

"Wait," said the guard. "The little deer must wait in a different area. We have an area for the mothers and fathers and another for the fawns."

Freckles began to cry and said that he didn't want to go. Hope put her head next to his and said, "Freckles, I will see you very soon and then we will go into the forest together."

Freckles and the other fawns were taken to another part of the forest. It was a big, gated area where there were lots of other little deer.

The next day, Hope asked to see Freckles. "Not today," said the guard. She went to him each day to ask about Freckles, but she always got the same answer: "Not today!"

The guard said to Hope, "I don't know when you can see Freckles. I am waiting to be told what to do. The General has to decide."

Time passed, then one day a guard told little Freckles that he and the other fawns were being taken to another place.

After a long ride, the guard took Freckles off of the big, cramped truck he had traveled in, and brought him to a family of deer who would take care of him until he and his momma could be reunited.

The mother of the family of deer said to Freckles, "Come with me, little one. We'll look after you. You can play with the other little deer and we'll feed you, too."

It was very pretty here, and Freckles thought to himself, *This must be the beautiful place my momma told me about.* Even though this new deer family was very nice to him, Freckles missed his mother so much.

A few days later, a guard came to see Hope. "The people who are in charge believe you when you say that the Olden Forest is dangerous. So, they decided that you can live in the Big Pine Forest after all."

Hope was so happy. "Will you bring me to Freckles now?"

The woman said that Freckles was staying with another family of deer and that she had to make arrangements to bring Freckles back to Hope.

All of a sudden, Hope heard the other deer crying out loud. A guard was telling them that they couldn't stay and that they had to go back home to their forests.

One deer cried to the guard, "No, don't take us back to our forests! It is too dangerous there!"

"I'm sorry, but the General decided that you can't stay in the Big Pine Forest," the guard replied.

"Wait, wait! Where are our children?" the other deer asked. The guard told them that their little fawns would be brought back to them at their forests very soon. The deer were crying as they got onto the truck without their children.

For weeks on end, Hope waited for Freckles to be brought back. Finally, she heard the voice she had been anticipating for so long.

"Momma, Momma, it's me, it's Freckles!" Hope ran to her little boy and nuzzled him with her nose.

The guard drove Hope and Freckles to another part of the beautiful forest where they could begin living in their new home together.

Each night, as Freckles was getting ready to sleep on the soft pine needles on the ground, Hope would say, "We are so blessed to be able to live in the Big Pine Forest. Freckles, remember to pray for all of the deer we met who had to go back to their forests."

As Freckles' eyes began to close, he snuggled next to his momma.

Hope looked at her little boy and said, "One day when you are all grown up, perhaps you can convince the people in this beautiful forest to let the other deer come to live here where they won't have to be afraid of the jaguars and the coyotes. You will have to convince the General that it is big enough to help many more."

Hope and Freckles met other deer from the Olden Forest, and many kinds of other animals who came from all different places.

It was a new beginning for Hope and Freckles in the Big Pine
Forest that they now called their home.

Useful Definitions for Young Readers

Refugee: Someone who has been forced to leave their country in order to escape war, persecution, or natural disaster.

Refugee Camp: A temporary settlement built to receive refugees. Refugee camps usually accommodate displaced persons who have fled their home country.

Asylum: Protection granted by a nation to someone who has left their native country as a political refugee.

Foreigner: Someone born in or coming from a country other than one's own.

Resources for Parents & Educators

Now that you've read the story of Hope and Freckles, continue to explore the plight of refugees and asylum seekers around the world. Homelessness, swindling by transporters, and a lack of acceptance due to fear of the foreigner are just some of the challenges faced by refugees and asylum seekers. Learn more at the book's website:

www.HopeAndFreckles.com

Questions for Discussion

Here are some questions that you might consider using to begin a dialogue about the book that you have just read.

1. Why did Hope and Freckles leave the Olden Forest?

2. When they reached the Big Pine Forest, why didn't the guards let them in?

3. How did you feel when Freckles had to leave his momma and go to stay in a different place?

4. What does the word "refugee" mean? Were Hope and Freckles refugees?

5. Do you know what the word "asylum" means? Did Hope seek asylum in the Big Pine Forest?

6. Did you feel sad when the other deer had to go back to their own forests without their children?

7. What do you think happens to Hope and Freckles in their new forest?

Watch for the next story in this series,

Hope and Freckles: Life in a New Forest

About the Author

Bill Kiley is a retired Deputy Police Chief and also a retired Colonel from the U.S. Army. A native of Brooklyn, New York, Bill resides on Long Island, New York, with his wife of forty-eight years, Kathy. Among his academic credentials, Bill Kiley holds two Master of Science degrees, is a graduate of the F.B.I. National Academy in Quantico, Virginia, and also the U.S. Army Command and General Staff College. Mr. Kiley has been an adjunct professor of Criminal Justice at Suffolk County Community College and at Long Island University. He is a Past President of the International Association for Property and Evidence, Inc. Bill has been a presenter and conducted training throughout the United States, Canada, and in Dubai (UAE). Additionally, Bill Kiley is the Past President of the New York State and Eastern Canada Chapter of the F.B.I. National Academy Associates. Mr. Kiley has been the recipient of numerous awards and recognitions throughout his various professional careers.

As the grandfather of five granddaughters, Bill knows the powerful impact that children's picture books can have on young minds. So, at seventy years of age, motivated by his heart and his head, Mr. Kiley decided to write a children's picture book that addresses the plight of refugees and asylum seekers throughout the world. His book, *Hope and Freckles: Fleeing to a Better Forest*, is the first of a planned series.